This book belongs to

....

This edition published by Parragon Books Ltd
in 2015 and distributed by

Parragon Inc.
440 Park Avenue South, 13th Floor
New York, NY 10016
www.parragon.com

Copyright © Parragon Books Ltd 2015

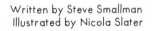

Written by Steve Smallman
Illustrated by Nicola Slater

Edited by Grace Harvey
Designed by Ailsa Cullen
Production by Charlotte McKillop

ISBN 978-1-4723-5097-8

Printed in China

SPOT A LOT VEHICLE ADVENTURE

AND COUNT A LITTLE, TOO!

STEVE SMALLMAN   NICOLA SLATER

PaRragon

Bath · New York · Cologne · Melbourne · Delhi
Hong Kong · Shenzhen · Singapore · Amsterdam

This package has
to get to town ...
But the delivery truck
has broken down!

TOWN

DEPOT

Find and follow the dog in every picture!

1 motorbike gives me a ride

Spot 2 motor scooters!

Find a car pulling a big trailer.

Where is the truck full of dirt?

in the sidecar
on the side!

This nice old car is waterproof,

Find 4 yellow umbrellas.

Spot a dog wearing an umbrella hat.

but look—
2 cars don't
have a roof!

Where is the open manhole?

The farmer's tractor rumbles on—

Find 2 dogs playing chase!

Spot 3 pink piglets.

but where have his **3** dirt bikes gone?

Where is the
horse hiding?

From this boat I see the trails

Where is my mermaid friend?

Find a message in a bottle.

Spot 4 little orange fish.

of **4** big boats with stripy sails!

Hot air balloons can't fly as fast

Can you see my 4 seagull friends?

as those **5** jet planes whizzing past!

Spot the balloon that looks like an elephant.

Find a brave little mouse!

6 yellow diggers
digging holes

Spot 3 gray wheelbarrows.

7 fire engines with screeching tires

Find the cat that's stolen my hat.

Find 3 lucky black cats.

rescue cats and
put out fires!

Spot a hot air balloon.

8 buses full of unwell pets

This bicycle ride
is a disaster—

Spot an orange car.

Find 3 circus trains.

From this submarine I spy

Spot 2 fish kissing!

Find 2 seahorses.

10 helicopters zooming by!

Can you see a green pufferfish?

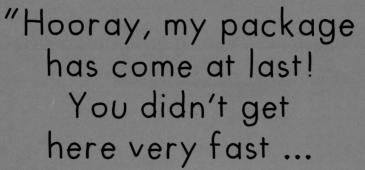

"Hooray, my package
has come at last!
You didn't get
here very fast ...